Professor Odd #10

PROFESSOR ODD
THE THOUSAND SONGS

Professor Odd #10

by
GOLDEEN OGAWA

a Heliopause Production

FICTION/Science Fiction, Adventure

FICTION/Fantasy, General

First Edition 2017

ISBN: 978-1-945781-04-9

Prologue

IT ALL BEGAN when Professor Odd came storming into the Oddity, up the stairs and past the cockpit, to stand at the head of the table. Alister and Elo had carved spaces out of the perpetual clutter on it in order to eat breakfast there, and they regarded her curiously as she raised her fist triumphantly into the air and declared:

"I *got* them!"

Alister and Elo stared at her. She was wearing her most colorful wig to date: a rainbow of orange and pink with streaks of sky blue. It should have clashed horribly with the rest of her clothes, but the royal blue trousers seemed to complement it, and her shirt, Alister noticed, was a matching light blue with pink buttons. He couldn't see much of it, however, because she was wearing a shiny orange coat over it. The only thing that didn't fit was the lime green scarf, but this was tucked mostly under her collar—leaving the tentacle that sprouted from the base of her skull to coil excitedly over one shoulder.

Alister swallowed a mouthful of porridge and asked: "Got what?"

"*Tickets!*" Professor Odd said, grinning hugely, her jaguar eyes gleaming.

"Tickets . . . for what?" Elo prodded, cautiously.

"The *show*, of course," said Professor Odd, doing a giggling dance at the head of the table. "You'll like it, I promise!"

"That's what you said about that planet with the Italian aliens," Alister pointed out. "And the beach with dinosaurs. And the nebula."

Professor Odd deflated a little. "Didn't you like them?" she asked, concerned.

"Well, yes," Alister admitted. "But the first time, we were attacked by robots from outer space. The second time, we got plopped in the middle of a political *and* natural disaster, and when we went to look at the nebula the spaceship we were on turned out to be lost in the wrong universe, and you were nearly killed!"

Professor Odd made a sound like "*Pffft,*" and flapped her hands at him. "That wasn't *on purpose,*" she insisted. "Those things *happen.* Sometimes. Not always. And it *shouldn't* happen this time. This world is quite stable—I made sure of it. And I've got *friends* there. And you won't have to pretend to be my guide dog," she added to Elo. "It's a borderline unconventional world, and they've seen stranger stuff in the last few years. Dave can come too, if he doesn't mind being mistaken for a robot, as usual."

"WHY WOULD I WISH TO GO, THEN?" Dave asked from the catwalk above them. Looking up, Alister saw him lounging on the railing, three bright green, yellow-tipped octopus arms wound securely around the beam. There was a flash of orange and gold as his single, huge eye blinked down at them. Tucked in amongst the fine, anemone-like filaments that covered his underside was a square gray box with some cables and a speaker. This was Dave's slime-to-audio translator, which he had to carry everywhere because his native language consisted of chemical changes in the psychoactive slime he oozed from every pore. It was a much more efficient way of communicating, especially if you lived in a liquid environment (which Dave preferred), but short of clamping himself physically over someone's head, the mechanical translator was the only way for Dave to "speak." It made him sound like an angry computer, and combined with the fact that his panvironment suit resembled a barrel with gears and a glass dome, decked with sensors, anti-grav plates, and flashing lights, it was understandable that people multiversally mistook him for a robot.

Since Dave was *actually* a bright green creature roughly the size and shape of a pie pan with ten arms, one large eye, countless underbelly tentacles and no recognizable brain, the misconception was something of a sore point with him.

"*Because,*" Professor Odd answered, her grin growing, if possible, even wider. "It's a *Princess Die* concert! She's got a new album out, and everything. It's going to be *marvelous!*"

"I'm sorry," said Alister, shaking his head a little. "*Who?*"

"Princess Die," said Professor Odd. "Dee, ai, eee, like 'to die.' But she hasn't yet, which is good, because it means we can go watch her perform. Her shows are great fun, *and . . .* " here Professor Odd actually clapped her hands to her cheeks and bounced up and down, her voice becoming an impossibly high squeal. " . . . *Extrascape* is opening for her! They've come back, just for this tour! You *have* to see them!"

Alister and Elo blinked at each other in confusion.

"You're certainly excited," the wolf said. "Are they very special then?"

Professor Odd dropped her hands like they had suddenly turned to lead bricks. "Didn't I *tell* you about Extrascape? The mad god? The thousand songs?"

Very slowly, her canine face blank, Elo shook her head.

Professor Odd let out a sound like "*Gh-huh!*" and flopped into the nearest chair. This brought the upper half of her figure in front of one of the Oddity's windows, which looked out on the void between universes, and gave her a surreal, multihued backdrop. She looked almost like a colorful tropical fish against the night beyond.

Heaving a sigh she kicked her feet up onto the table, and knitting her fingers together, she said, "Well, we do have time. I suppose I should tell you about them. Care to listen, Dave? You might find this rather interesting!"

There was some squelching, and then the reply came:

"I HAVE SATISFACTORY AUDIO RECEPTION FROM MY CURRENT LOCATION, THANK YOU."

Professor Odd shrugged.

"Right then," she said. "Since you haven't even heard of Princess Die—she must have gone by a different name in your world, Alister—I'd better start a little before the beginning and tell you about her. Because she's very important. Right. So you know how some performing artists won't use their real names? She's one of those. Only Princess Die has sort of *become* her real name, and that's what I've always called her. I first heard her music, my, my . . . a long time ago now, and quite by accident. That doesn't really matter though. What matters is that I liked her songs so much that I took the Oddity and snuck in to one of her concerts. I didn't know it then, but that concert was rather a big deal: she'd been having problems, and her managers were trying to give her one of those 'reboots' they do with artists. As if you could fix them by turning them off and on again, like a computer." Professor Odd snorted disdainfully. "Anyway, it was a big to-do at a famous club in a large city—but because one of Princess Die's trademarks was her wild costumes, most of the attendees were *also* dressed a little . . . well . . . a little *oddly.* So for once I fit right in without trying."

Professor Odd grinned in an inward sort of way, clearly relishing the memory. "I remember it was hot, and stuffy, and they'd set up a laser light show to go along with the music. It *should* have been tacky and annoying, but combined with everything else—with the music and the costumes and the audience all clapping and cheering . . . well, it was really quite marvelous. And then, right in the middle of it all—just as she was getting to the end of one of her best songs—she vanished. Poof. Gone. There was a puff of smoke and everything, and all the lights went out."

Alister blinked. "You mean, she disappeared as part of her act?"

"*Noooooo . . .* " said Professor Odd, her eyes wide and earnest. "Not at *all* part of her act! I mean, people thought it was for about five minutes, but then they got bored and started asking questions. Someone turned on the house lights, and her security—big people in black clothes—went up on stage and started looking around, and her dancers all sort of shuffled off to the side and stood there, looking confused and helpless. And they couldn't find her *anywhere*."

"And what did *you* do?" Elo asked.

Professor Odd grinned at them. "What do you *think* I did?"

Part One

"I RAN AS FAST AS I COULD for the Oddity, of course. Had to wrestle my way through the crowd and into the hallway. Good thing I'd left the portal so close, really. Everyone was confused and some people were panicking. Once I got back, I immediately ran a sweep for other transdimensional activity. It was a bit of a long shot, since this universe was fairly conventional back then, but it paid off! I'd barely started the sweep when the Oddity went agog with lights: she'd found a *rift*. A major rift in the fabric of the universe. Dangerous things, they are, but this one had been stitched shut again almost immediately, so there had been no excess damage.

"I disconnected the Oddity and did a search of nearby universes for one containing an alien—er, that is, a person from a different universe. And not only did I find one . . . I found one containing *multiple* aliens, all from *different universes* from *each other*. There was this little island where a whole bunch of people from different universes were all crowded together. Tightly. It looked suspicious even from that distance, and when I brought the Oddity in closer I saw that universe was *riddled* with stitched rifts.

"I'd like to say I took a break at this point and examined the situation more closely, but you have to understand that I was younger then—this was before I even met Elo!—and I was still getting to know the Oddity. So I simply opened the door nearest to where Princess Die was and went running out, not knowing what I would find on the other side.

"I came through into a place that felt like a *furnace.* I was on this narrow metal walkway with thin, cable railings, and the floor was a grate through which I could see more walkways crisscrossing beneath me, down and down, until they were lost in a haze of steam. The whole place was monstrously hot, and the lights were all orange or red. It looked a little like being suspended over the mouth of a volcano, but not *that* hot—obviously.

"Anyway, the whole thing was roughly tube-shaped, with little doors set at intervals along the wall, and a big column up the center that looked like a track for some sort of elevator car. I turned right around again and found that the Oddity had used one of those doors as an anchor. The doors on either side were locked, so I banged on both, trying to get a response. There was none from either, and I was just considering how I would go about picking the lock when the elevator car turned up, hissing to a stop on my level, and a couple people got out.

"I say they were people, but that doesn't mean they were *human,* you understand. These folks looked a bit more like praying mantises . . . with thin, sticky legs and fat abdomens. They also had a third set of appendages behind their shoulders that sort of zigzagged into these huge, single-digit pincers. Like, if you hold your hand up so it's level with your shoulder and bend it down, and pretend that your fingers are fused together and reach *back* down to your elbow—that's sort of what these arms looked like. I think they were what put me in mind of praying mantises, really, because they were the same shape as a mantis claw.

"They were wearing dark uniforms and helmets, so I couldn't see their faces, and each one carried a set of chains with clasps on the end, like collars. I decided I didn't want them to see me, so I hurried along the catwalk to a little crevice between some pipes and squeezed in between them. From there I heard the mantis people walk over to one of the doors I'd been banging on—*clickity-clack,* just like giant insects—and they opened the door, which creaked. One of them went inside, and I heard the collars snap onto something, and then there was more clicking as they walked back to the elevator, and when I leaned around to look I saw they were leading someone between them. Someone tall and slender with long, lavender hair, who they'd apparently dressed in a white paper slip—like a stiff hospital gown.

"It was Princess Die, of course, but she didn't look like herself. Not the lavender hair, mind you—that was the same as when I'd last seen her—but she walked kind of blindly, and when she had to turn onto the catwalk to the elevator it was this sharp right-angle, not natural. It was like something else was making her move.

"I knew I couldn't just barge in and rescue her—the mantis people were bigger than me, and besides, they had extra collars. I had my sword-cane with me, but I also didn't want to *hurt* anyone. Not unless I had to. So I waited until they were safely in the elevator, and then I skipped back to the Oddity and brought up a schematic of the whole place—which was what I should have done in the first place.

"It turned out the tube where I'd come through was just one of a dozen towers, all connected at their base by a network of underground tunnels, which converged in the form of a giant, underground ring consisting of a lot of rooms with electrical generators, a structure that looked like a sort of hospital, and one big, spherical room with a single chair in the middle. All this was under an arena of sorts, with a huge circular grandstand and *something* suspended over it. I say *something* because even the Oddity couldn't make out what it was, and at the time I was more interested in the spherical room, because that was where they'd taken Princess Die.

"Now, I wish I could tell you I'd done something *clever,* like figured out how she was likely to exit that room, and then put the Oddity on standby so that the portal would activate the moment she passed through . . . but this was a long time ago, and I didn't know the Oddity so well back then. So I opened the door onto a ventilation duct—just big enough for me to peer through—and listened in on what was happening.

"The mantis people had sat her in a chair like the kind you find at the dentist's. It was on a hydraulic lift and held Princess Die at about head height. From my vantage point I could see her collar, which was a thin strip of silver metal with little bulbs of glass on either side. These were blinking, slowly, with purple light. A cord led out from the back of the collar, trailing over the chair to a plug in the floor. Over to one side, in a little cube of glass, was a mantis person dressed like a medical technician: all stiff, white folds. They were also wearing a helmet with a visor, but from what I could see their face looked surprisingly humanoid—only gray-blue, not pink-brown. They were typing away with their stick-like hands, with their shoulder arms folded tightly at their sides.

"Then, all at once, a jumble of mechanized arms descended from the ceiling and spread out over Princess Die. There was a whirring, and green lasers shot from the tips. These passed back and forth over her body, side-to-side, like the toner head of an inkjet printer, and with each swipe her clothes changed. Line by line, the outfit she'd been wearing in the club was erased, and behind it was printed a sheer, black garment like a bathing suit, with big, triangular mirrors decorating the left shoulder.

"It reminded me very much of an outfit she'd worn in one of her early videos, right around the time she became really famous. It was puzzling, but what was even more distressing was that she didn't seem to be restrained in any way—except for the collar. I kept trying to get her attention—I knew I was in her line of sight, because I could see her eyes—but she just stared past me at the ceiling.

"After a while, when the lasers finished printing her new clothes, the chair changed shape so she was in an upright sitting position, then descended until her feet touched the ground. Then more arms appeared out of hidden holes in the floor and printed shoes—really amazing shoes, like crystal, with immensely tall heels—onto her feet. More lasers restyled her hair, and some specialized arms sprayed her face with a fine powder that formed into eye shadow and mascara and lipstick. They'd changed her hair color to turquoise, like it had been in the video, with matching lipstick and warm, red eye shadow. Finally the tech came over and unplugged her collar, and Princess Die sat up and looked around.

"I kept hoping she'd panic, or show some sign that she realized what was happening to her, but she didn't. She looked right at the mantis person's humanoid-but-not-human face and didn't react at all. She let them help her out of the chair, and followed them out of the room.

"As soon as they were gone I recalibrated the Oddity's door to let into the little cubicle. I wanted to see if I could figure out what they'd done to her, but the controls were labeled in a language I didn't recognize. It didn't look like mind control, though, so I assumed that must have something to do with the collar she was wearing. Then I looked out into the room, and up at the ceiling—and finally saw what Princess Die had been staring at the whole time.

"Directly above the chair where Princess Die had lain there was a video screen, and on it was a series of images depicting various musicians performing in front of huge, cheering crowds. I couldn't make sense of it, which bothered me. Now it's so obvious I don't understand why I didn't see the reason, but that's experience for you.

"You'll laugh, but this was when I began to get *really* curious about what was going on. Before, I just wanted to get my favorite musician back. Now I wanted to *understand* what was happening. Because, just from looking at the whole setup the mantis people had built, and the way they all seemed to be going about their business like this was something they did *every day*, it was obvious that Princess Die was not the first person they'd kidnapped . . . and she wouldn't be the last, either, if I didn't do something about it.

"I fetched a multiversal translator from the Oddity, and while it was working on the controls inside the cubicle I carefully locked all the doors, so I wouldn't be interrupted. I had that much sense, at least. I remember everything was very clean and smooth and well maintained, and there were lots of little cameras, now I looked, which I belatedly went around and switched off.

"By the time I'd finished, so was the translator, and when I went back into the cubicle I found that the controls mostly had to do with the lasers that disintegrated and reintegrated Die's clothes. I left them alone, and went for the little computer terminal that had access to the building's mainframe. From there I was able, with some careful fiddling, to gain access to the network of cameras that fairly blanketed the place. And what I found . . . well . . . it wasn't at all *nice.*

"The tubular silos where Die had originally been kept were only about half full . . . but they were filled with *people.* And not just any people. *Multiples* of the same person from different universes! Some of them I didn't recognize, but a few names I did. There were two David Joneses and *four* George O'Dowds *and* a Robyn Fenty and almost a dozen Rose Seberts. Which, by the way, are all notable musicians and singers—though you might not know them by those names. Going through the list, I found enough of them that I guessed the rest were probably kidnapped musicians as well.

"And then I found a directory labeled '*Discontinued Series.*' That's right, '*Discontinued Series,*' like these people were a toy or motor car that the company had stopped producing. And those names . . . *those* names gave me pause.

"The first on the list was *Amy Jade Winehouse.* Then there was Roger Barrett, Dana Haughton, Kurt Donald Kobain, and a long list of others. Farrokh Bulsara, who is better known in most of his universes as *Freddie Mercury,* was about halfway down. And then, right at the bottom, were three names very close together, and then one more. These were Janis Lyn Joplin, James Marshall Hendrix, Alan Christie Wilson, and finally Lewis Brian Hopkins Jones. Which won't mean anything to you unless you are familiar with popular North American musicians of the third quarter of the twentieth century A.D. Which, as it happened, I *was.*

"It made me forget almost entirely about Princess Die. Because the first thing I can tell you about all the people listed under '*Discontinued Series*' is that they were, in the vast majority of their universes, *dead.* In the case of Joplin, Hendrix, Wilson and Jones, they had died over the course of about a year relative to each other. They were all twenty-seven, too, which doesn't mean anything, really, except that some people seem to think it does. Which it *did,* but not what they thought.

"It *meant* something *was* killing these people. Maybe it looked like drugs or disease or even murder to the natives of their home universes, but I was convinced all their deaths were linked to whatever was going on here, in this distant world.

"Then my line of reasoning jumped forward, and I remembered universes where certain musicians died earlier, or later, or not at all. And I realized that wasn't just because of randomness and differences between worldtracks—it was because not all of those people had been kidnapped yet! And, what was perhaps worst, they now had my favorite musician of them all.

"It made me sick. It made me *furious.* But under all that, I still wondered *why?* To run a transuniversal kidnapping operation would require a *huge* amount of energy and resources. So these mantis folk—or whoever was in charge—*must* have a good reason.

"And that's when I went back to the blueprints of the building and figured out what it was. It only took a little bit of turning about, and then the image was, like I mentioned before, *obvious.*

"It was a *stadium.* The kind with a grandstand all the way around, and we were under the ground beneath it, and there were elevator shafts leading up and down, and the silos were linked by underground rail lines. Above it . . . well, the schematics didn't show anything above the grandstands, but there was an illustration for the thing that had confused the Oddity.

"It was as if two giant arches had been built over the stadium, so they crossed in the center, and from these arches hung a net that covered the center of the stadium. From the junction of the arches hung a kind of . . . well . . . I suppose you could call it a *gun.* It was only a gun in that it shot things, however. I don't think it was ever meant to be a weapon. I recognized lasers, and some things that looked like proton accelerators but probably weren't. They were meant for shooting very small, very dense particles, I could tell that much.

"This whole contraption was pointed down at the net, which looked a little odd from the blueprints, but without seeing it in person I couldn't tell what it was.

"It was around then I began hearing things—pounding feet outside the door, clicking voices—and decided it was time to move on. I hopped back into the Oddity, disconnected, and re-connected at an out-of-the-way maintenance hatch at the base of the grandstand.

"I stepped out and got hit by the noise. That's what it felt like, anyway. Roars and cheers and a high buzzing sound. Underneath all that was a steady, heavy beat of a bass that vibrated the air and the concrete walls around me, and through it all were faint wisps of music, but I could barely make them out.

"Looking around, I found I was in a small tunnel that led under a block of seats and out onto the field—which was built up with a stage on lots of stilts with lights and fog machines underneath. Behind me was a sort of thoroughfare, but access was blocked by a fence made of silver wire, which suited me just fine. I went the other way, toward the stage, and climbed up next to one of the lights—a big thing, wider than my arms could reach—and looked around.

"I could barely see the roaring crowd, but from the few I glimpsed, peeking over a high parapet and far in the distance, up near the canopy, they looked more human than anyone else I'd seen in the world, save Princess Die herself. They were all dressed in exciting outfits with lots of face paint, but they were unmistakably *human*.

"This really confused me for a moment, but then I caught a flicker—almost unnoticeable unless you looked closely—and suddenly all the little wrong things about the crowd stood out glaringly. The fact that *all* the members that I could see were more or less the same ideal shape. At the real concert I had seen fat people, thin people, tall people, short people, old, young, and all sorts of combinations. *These* people were more or less the same size and shape, with only minimal effort given to making them appear male or female, and all had a plasticky agelessness that was a little creepy. And—and this was something that had struck me as wrong from the very beginning—the crowd had a strange look to it like there were patches of more green or blue or black. Not like blocks of color, you understand, just like a group of people who were wearing *mostly* black—or green or blue. And I realized the reason I was noticing these collections was because they were arranged in a perfect, repeating *pattern*. Like the pattern on a carpet or a tablecloth. That is to say, the *crowd* was made up of maybe fifty or so unique individuals, which had just been copied until they filled the stadium. Combined with the flicker I'd seen earlier, this made me realize they weren't real people at all, and I looked around for something that might be projecting the image.

"That's when I looked up and saw the gun for the first time in person. It looked a lot smaller than on the blueprint, being suspended hundreds of feet in the air, and it was further hidden by the colored lasers that were shooting down onto the stage, but I guessed that was where they'd put the projectors.

"Projectors to create the visual illusion of a packed house of excited fans, with speakers hidden in the grandstand to make the cheering, the entire thing was . . .

"Well, it was a *show*. But not a show for any audience. There *was no* audience.

"Then I caught movement under the stage, and a trapdoor opened, and the noise from the stands tripled as Princess Die was raised into view.

"She was wearing the same outfit I'd seen them print onto her, a headset microphone, and the silver collar with flashing purple bulbs. She swelled up at the sight of the crowd, coming alive for the first time, and I saw her inhale deeply.

"That's when I realized the whole thing was back to front. The fake audience was the show *for her*. *She* was its audience. Which made no sense at all. Unless there was *another* audience. A hidden audience. Something watching her being watched. So why did they need the fake audience in the first place? For the same reason they needed the giant stadium and the powerful sound system and the lights and the lasers and the smoke. To make her *feel* like it really was a stage, so she would give a real performance.

"It's a well known fact that performers—actors, singers, musicians, anyone who gets up on a stage to entertain people, really—draw energy from their audience. All that enthusiasm pouring out from people buoys them up, makes them give bigger, better performances. *That's* what the audience was for. I just didn't know what *Princess Die's* performance was for . . .

"I didn't have time to think all this, in order, just then. It sort of happened at the back of my head while I was watching Princess Die look around, square her shoulders, and march down the stage to where a grand piano, covered in mirrors, had been set up. As she went she began to speak, welcoming the audience (which wasn't actually there) and telling them how excited she was to sing for them.

"It was the exact same speech she'd given at the beginning of her last performance . . . back in the club . . . the one she had been abducted in the middle of.

"It was—and you know I don't use this term lightly—one of the *oddest* things I'd ever seen. I stood there, holding onto the side of the light, and just stared as she threw a leg over the piano bench, sat down, and began to play.

"She played quite well. You'd never have guessed she had been abducted, drugged, and brainwashed. The song she played was one of her ballads, all slow and throaty. Not my favorite, but she performed it well. I had to tear my eyes away from her to look up, though, because something was happening with the gun hanging above her.

"I really didn't like the look of it. I didn't like that I couldn't tell what some of the barrels were for, and I didn't like how it was pointed directly at the stage. I also didn't like how the biggest barrel, the one ringed by lasers, was beginning to belch a kind of steam. I say a *kind* of steam, because it *kind* of looked like steam, but wasn't. It was too . . . too *stringy*. And it fell in waves that stretched and formed into gossamer fine strands, like spiderwebs floating on wind.

"These strands slowly sank, until they pillowed on the net below the gun, and collected there, growing denser and denser. Their color kept changing, from purple to blue and then black and back to purple again. At first I thought it was the lights making them change. I was wrong, but I didn't find out until later.

"Staring upward, I finally noticed the little screen attached to the side of the gun. It had a digital readout that said 'Sacrifice of Song' in the native's language, and under that the numeral '1', followed by a slash, then another '1', a comma, and three 'o's. One out of one thousand . . . somethings. Songs, I guessed, when Princess Die finished her first song and moved on to the next. Then the first numeral flickered, and became a two. Two out of one thousand. I wondered what would happen when she reached a thousand songs . . . assuming she could even perform that many in one sitting. Unless it didn't have to be in one sitting.

"I decided I didn't want to wait around to find out. The Oddity was nearby, and so was Princess Die. I had my trusty sword-cane, and I couldn't see any mantis people. So I hopped down off the huge light, climbed up onto the stage, and ran across it toward the woman sitting at the piano.

"I made it . . . *oooh,* about halfway, before a few guards showed up. Several, actually. They came swarming over the edge of the stage, all dressed in black, with their third appendages snapping like wings.

"Princess Die didn't seem to notice them. She noticed me, because I managed to reach her and take hold of her collar by one purple bulb. It zapped me. As I swore and shook my hand she stood up, turned around and glared at me. It's funny to think of it now, but she was absolutely *furious.*

"'*Excuse me,*' she said. 'This is very *rude* of you!'

"I'd never had to apologize to the person I was rescuing before. It struck me dumb. Also, I was standing *right next* to Princess Die, of all people, and my heart was pounding from nerves. I couldn't think what to say, and I was so embarrassed I just cackled, and said the first thing that came into my head:

"'You've got to get the collar off. That's what's keeping you from remembering—I think!'

"She just stared at me, her eyes wide. I could really see the makeup around them. From a distance it all blended into her face and made her look like some supernatural creature, but up close she was just a woman with a lot of paint on. It made her even more amazing, in a way. She was suddenly, urgently *real* in a way that helped calm my nerves a bit. Princess Die was an awful lot of things to me, but at that moment she was mainly a human being, in over her head in trouble, and she needed my help. Whether she knew it or not.

"'Come *on*,' I said, reaching for her arm. 'I'll explain on the way home!'

"But she stood there like a rock, staring at me in disbelief, and the mantis people closed in around us.

"They seemed not to want to touch Princess Die, which bought me a little more time. I leaned in close and whispered to her: 'There is a collar around your neck, you *need* to take it off. Also, there is a *gun* pointed at this stage and I don't like what's coming out of it.'

"This seemed to get through to her. She looked up for the first time, saw the mouth of the largest barrel, now almost entirely obscured by the thick tendrils of purple, blue, and black smoke, then looked back down again and saw the mantis people. I think it was the first time she noticed them. She frowned and wrinkled her nose and said, '*What . . . ?*' and took a step back.

"Then the mantis people were on me, and I was kicking and lashing out with my cane and trying to keep ahold of Princess

Die . . . but she was surrounded by mantis people in seconds, and I was forced backward, off the stage.

"Someone caught the end of my cane and nearly unsheathed the sword. I yanked it back, and began looking for an escape. There was no way of getting through the crowd, but I knew there were trapdoors under the stage, if only I could find one. The floor was smooth, but by stamping and listening I was able to find one—still beating back guards as I shuffled around the stage—and by sheer luck there was a little recessed switch in the floor next to it which opened it. Right out from under my feet.

"I dropped, landed *hard* on the concrete beneath the stage, and found myself in a maze of huge pipes. One of them was marked with a pictogram of a mantis person throwing something that looked like crumpled paper into a chute. Garbage disposal, I presumed, so I went over and opened the hatch in the side. It smelled tangy, but not bad. And it was big enough for me to fit. And it led *away* from the huge swarm of mantis people.

"I didn't think. I jumped. Vaulted into the pipe, and began to slide. Then the pipe turned, and I went into free fall. And that, my friends, is when things began to get *interesting.*"

The Oddity made a chirping noise, not unlike a bird, making Alister start. He had become so absorbed in Professor Odd's story that he found he was gripping the table in his anxiety.

"And *then* what?" Elo yelped.

"I just realized something," Professor Odd said, a worried frown growing over her brow.

"What?" asked Alister.

Professor Odd looked up at him. "I'm *hungry.*"

"I think we have some leftover meatloaf," Elo offered, but Professor Odd shook her head.

"*Meatloaf* before Princess Die? No, no, no, that will not *do*. The show is in San Jose this time, we are *not* eating *meatloaf!*" She was rummaging in the pockets of her coat as she spoke, and now produced a small, blue card—it looked a bit like a credit card to Alister, but it was longer and narrower. She tapped it on the table, rubbed it on her sleeve, and squinted at it critically. Then her expression cleared, and she smiled.

"Oh, this is *more* than enough. *Bless* Jill. Do either of you feel like a nice dinner before the concert? There is a *wonderful* little bar where they serve sushi instead of alcohol. It's extra friendly, so you can come as you are."

"Sorry?" said Elo. "What does *extra* friendly mean? Are they so friendly they won't mind a talking dog and a tentacle monster in a barrel?"

Professor Odd waved her hand. "It's native slang. *Extra*-ordinaries, is what they call creatures like . . . well, creatures like *you*. This universe is rather special that way. So . . . would you like to come? Though we could always order out I suppose . . . "

She trailed off, looking woebegone. Elo rolled her eyes. "Of *course* we'll come," she said.

Professor Odd grinned expansively, and five minutes later they were tramping down the steps of the Oddity and out onto a cement walkway beside a wide road. It was evening, and tall buildings were just lighting up against the dim purple sky. There was an immediate sound of car engines and the distant blare of a train, and for one moment it was so bone-achingly ordinary Alister thought he was back in his home universe.

Then something loomed past them that was *not* a car. It had long legs, and moved rather like a horse, and there was a shining horn on its head. It glowed orange and yellow, a strand of light like a flowing tail trailing behind it.

"What was *that?*" Alister gasped.

"What?" said Professor Odd. "Oh, that was a unicorn. They like using the roads around here. Harmless, as long as *you* don't hurt *them.* Akairyu Sushi is this way, come on. I'll tell you the next bit while we walk. It's good, you'll like it."

They had barely gotten five yards, however, before the door to the Oddity (which was currently the chain-link gate to a junk-yard's back lot) flew open again and Dave trundled out, sloshing rather as his suit adjusted to the sidewalk.

"I WILL ACCOMPANY YOU," he stated, his antigravity plates giving out a small blast that sent him sailing sedately toward them.

"So you *were* listening," Elo said.

Dave didn't answer, but rolled patiently behind them while Professor Odd led the way down the street, under a raised free-way (cars, unseen, roared by overhead, rendering all conver-sation pointless). Once they were clear, and had passed onto quieter streets, Professor Odd continued her story.

"Yes, I fell. Plummeted, really. Down the tube. Not pleas-ant. I lost track of my cane, and heard it clattering away below me. That was distressing. That cane was *important* to me, you understand. But I couldn't very well let myself continue falling. Who *knew* what was at the bottom! Actually, I could guess. Excrement. Biological or otherwise. Either way I didn't want to hit it at speed. I didn't want to hit it *period.* So I stuck out both my legs and my hands . . . which of course just tipped me backward. Luckily the shaft was narrow enough my shoulders caught on the wall and, braced three ways, first I slowed, then skidded, and finally came to a complete stop.

"I hung there, listening to my heart pound, and the clattering of my cane growing more and more distant, until it disappeared into a faint splash.

"Considering the probable velocity of a tumbling cane down a vertical chute I calculated that I was maybe one hundred meters above the liquid into which my cane had fallen—and as I had no idea how deep or of what consistency it was, I judged it best to let myself down slowly, inch by inch.

"This took a long time, as you can imagine, and my back got quite sore and every part of me that touched the sides of the shaft got rather slimy. Luckily it wasn't so slimy as to completely destroy friction, and I was able to chimney down without slipping.

"I did wonder, in passing, how I would get back up. But since I knew the top of that shaft would be watched by mantis people, I figured it was better to go all the way down and then find another way. So. Down it was. Down, down, down, down, *down* . . . until my ankles and hands were as sore as my back, and the slime had seeped through to my knees and shoulders and halfway up my sleeves.

"And then I slid a foot down, and the shaft abruptly vanished, leaving my foot kicking at thin air. It was a close thing, but I managed to keep from falling by bracing my back against one side and my remaining foot against the other. I folded myself in half and peered down around my legs, trying to get a glimpse of what lay below.

"This was almost impossible because it was dark as a cave down there—had been in the shaft as well—but there was the faintest of faint red glows outlining the end of the tunnel, now I concentrated to look. There was also a weak updraft that smelled, thankfully, not of biological decomposition, but of algae and, again, that tangy smell—which by now I thought was some kind of metal cleaner. Lacking my cane, I chose to sacrifice my wig and, plucking it from my head, let it fall. Sooner rather than later, there was a little, wet, *plop.*

"The updraft made it difficult to judge, but I guessed the drop was less than twenty feet. Short enough to jump, and even if the water was only a few feet deep I stood a good chance of making it without any broken bones, assuming I landed properly. So I maneuvered myself around as best I could, and then dropped, feet first, out of the shaft. I tried to keep my body as relaxed as possible, which wasn't very, I'm afraid.

"Fortunately the water was deep. I went in all at once and plunged down . . . *far* down . . . into cold depths that closed in around me and tried to hold me. So I wriggled out of my coat, kicked off my shoes, and swam back up to the surface.

"I came up spitting and gasping and absolutely determined to go back down again and fetch my cane. This took several tries, and by the time I finally succeeded I was cold and shivering and exhausted—and I had lost my coat and shoes. Luckily the water reflected some of the dim, red light, and by it I could just make out a huge mound of something rising up out of the water. So I made for that, paddling as best I could with one hand, and pretty soon I reached an uneasy mountain of . . . well, it was junk, really. I clambered up on top of it, nearly losing my limbs several times in the cracks between old pieces of molding, pipes, and metal struts.

"I climbed just far enough to get entirely out of the water, and then laid myself out across the pokey heap. I wasn't exactly in *despair,* you understand. Still not as bad as being strapped to a table without any legs. But it was *discouraging,* and I was tired. I lay there in the almost complete darkness and closed my eyes, feeling the cold from my wet clothes begin to seep into my bones . . . and *that's* when the music started. Oh, here we are!"

While she spoke Professor Odd had led them down a busy city street with towering buildings on either side, across a small plaza with a cinema on one side and a park on the other, and finally down a narrow street lined with trees. Here all the ground-floor properties were occupied by various kinds of restaurants; Chinese, Indian, Greek and Italian were all represented. There was also an Irish pub and a late-night café where crowds of people sat, typing away at laptops. A flickering sign above a recessed door that claimed it to be "Hel's Kitchen" made Alister feel vaguely uncomfortable. Just beyond it, however, was a brightly lit storefront with strings of yellow lights inside paper lanterns. The name was in the kind of pictograph writing Alister could never make sense of, but above it was a bright red dragon arched over the door, and it was to this sign that Professor Odd had led them.

The small Asian woman behind the little podium just inside the door looked tired, but her face brightened immediately at the sight of Professor Odd.

"Irashai! *Irashai* Oddo-san!" she cried out, bobbing up and down in excitement. *"Ninzuu ha nan nin desu ka?"*

Professor Odd smiled, held up four fingers, and replied, *"Yon-tsu,"* and then continued on in far more rough, but no less enthusiastic, Japanese.

The result was they were led at once to a quiet table in the back that was almost a booth, the walls around it were so high. The table was dark brown wood, polished to a mirror shine, and the placemats were made of woven bamboo. There was a narrow vase with a single sprig of cherry blossoms in the center, and on the wall above them hung a painting of a hoofed creature that seemed to be part snake and part billowing cloud. Alister had no sooner picked up the menu—which was mostly in Japanese but thankfully had lots of pictures—when there was a rumbling growl and the tramp of heavy feet and he looked up to find a large man with pale gray skin wearing a dirty apron standing next to their table. At least, Alister assumed it was male. It was hard to tell, since the person's head was that of an octopus, with eight curling tentacle-arms sprouting from where his mouth should have been (might still *have* been, under all those suckers) and a large, domed head—on top of which was perched a neat blue cap.

"Tako-chan!" Professor Odd shouted joyously, and Alister watched in bemusement as she managed to shake one of the person's mouth-arms with her own tentacle. There was another exchange in Japanese, and then the octopus-man lumbered away again.

"WHO WAS THAT?" Dave demanded.

"Tako-chan," said Professor Odd, as if this explained everything. "He's the owner. One of them, anyway. I just ordered. Don't worry, you'll *like* it." She sipped the water that had been set out for them, and sighed. "Now . . . where was I?"

"You said you heard music?" Elo reminded her.

"*Ooooh* yes of course!" said Professor Odd, her eyes misting over as she leaned back in her seat. "Yes, yes, that music was *very* interesting.

"It was so unexpected, for a start. I could tell it wasn't echoing down from the stage above—it sounded as though it was coming just from the other side of the mountain I lay on. It was . . . synthetic sounding, full of beeps and whistles and a pulsing buzz like the beat of a drum. It was . . . well, it was actually very nice, in its own way. So after listening for a while, curiosity got the better of me, and I dragged myself up and over to get a better look at where it was coming from.

"What I found on the other side was absolutely *marvelous* . . . At first I was a little confused, I'll grant you, since it looked for a moment like I'd stumbled back into the Oddity.

"There were *lights,* little ones, blinking everywhere. They formed the shape of a rough tunnel leading up out of the water— I could tell because the surface reflected the lights back up at the ceiling—at the end of which was a great big circular light, which flashed dimly every time there was a drumbeat. Er, buzz-beat.

"The walls and ceiling of the tunnel were covered in pipes, which must have been glass because they would also glow with respect to certain notes. Red and purple and blue and green— all represented different tones of beats and whistles. And something about the way this was so specific and consistent—green lit up *only* for a particular instrument, with different greens for different notes—that I got the impression the sounds were coming *from* the lights, not just flashing on cue.

"It was fascinating music, too, now I was listening properly. It should have been repetitive and mind-numbing, but there was variation under the repetition that seemed to be building toward something. My brain got interested following the narrative of the music, and at the same time the beat was so powerful and energizing it made me forget, for a little while, that I was cold and tired and wet.

"I half climbed, half slid down the back side of the mountain, and found myself knee-deep in water with a smooth, concrete floor beneath. Slowly I waded up the tunnel, my head tilted back to watch the light show produced by the music.

"It was amazing. Interspersed between the pipes were little bulbs—those were the blinking lights I'd seen first—with squares of light behind them that changed color with the chord progression.

"Then the music began to fade, and with it the lights, until I was left stranded in silent darkness, the water just over my ankles.

"'Hello?' I called experimentally.

"The response was a run of sharp notes down the wall next to me, which appeared as a single white light dropping between bulbs. It repeated, moving down the tunnel, until it stopped and the music began again—but different this time. And by its light I saw someone standing a little ways up the tunnel, looking down at me.

"I only glimpsed them for a moment, and then the music changed and they were lost to darkness, and when that area was lit again they were gone. I knew what I had seen, though: a medium-sized, thinnish person in black leather, with a very strange head. It was too small to be a human head—though they were otherwise human-shaped—and lumpy with little colored lights down either side of what would have been their jaw, if they'd had one.

"Then I caught movement out of the corner of my eye, and I thought they had reappeared—except this was a *different* person: shorter, with a tapered waist, and the lights on their head ran up in two lines from where their eyes should have been. I say *should* because, from what I caught of their face, they didn't *have* eyes where a human would. Instead there was a big lens in the middle, with two smaller ones on either side, and a bunch more in a line underneath these. They were supported by piece of metal like a rectangular chin, that had a depression front and center like a speaker. That was all I could make out before *that* person disappeared as well.

"'Who are you?' I called out into the music, but my voice got eaten up in the notes. I thought they wouldn't have heard, but then, to my surprise, the *music* started talking. You know how, with the right pitch and tone, a musical note can almost sound like a word? Well, this was that, only *more* so. It was difficult to understand, but the words were few and far apart, so I had time to puzzle them out.

"'Weeeeeeeeeeee . . . are. The. Roooooooooooooooo . . . bots.'" Professor Odd sang the words in a hard, vibrating voice. "'Weeeeeeeeeeee . . . runnnnnnnnn . . . awaaaaaaaaay . . .'

"'Runaway robots?' I asked. 'That's fine with me, I ran away too. Er, what are you doing here?'

"'*Weeeeeeeeeeee . . . maaaaaaaake*—sorry, is that getting annoying? I'll talk normally then. Anyway, they said: 'We make *music*. We have no heart but a four-four beat. We are the robots who open up the extrascape.' Then the short one with the tapered waist reappeared at the end of the tunnel, silhouetted against the pulsing light there. I saw them bend down, rather stiffly, and pick up something off the ground. It was a helmet, I realized. Like a motorcycle helmet but with wires and cables hanging out the bottom instead of a chinstrap. The figure slipped it on over its head, fiddled with the wires, and then the helmet lit up with the same lights as were underneath it.

"'Two, zero, two,' said the music. 'Single B.'

Then the other figure—the one I'd seen first—stepped up next to them. They looked a lot taller, but I realized this was because they were wearing boots with heels almost as high as the ones Princess Die wore. They also picked up a helmet—this one had a big, bubble-like visor that reached back over the head, and had lights along the side to match the ones on the robot's jaw. When it was in place, the music said: 'Seven, one, three, D, H, C.'

"The chords grew louder, and in a crescendo the music said:

"'Together we are robots. Together we are *Extrascape.*'

"After that they stood there, looking at me blankly, and the music lulled. I realized they were waiting for me.

"I'm Professor Odd," I told them. "No numbers—not anymore. Just O, D, D. I'm afraid I'm a bit lost. Do you know if there's a way back up from here?'

"The music's lull faded into nothing, until the only light came from the robots' helmets—and the faint glow from the lamp behind them. It emitted a low hum, I realized, that never entirely went away.

"'Go back . . . *uuuuuuup?*' asked 202-B—the one with flat-soled boots and vertical lights. Their voice was quiet and granulated, and even though they were definitely *speaking*—not singing—every word they said *slid* into a note.

"'Yes, up,' I said. 'To the surface. The place with the arena. There's someone up there who's in trouble, and I need to rescue her.'

"'Up is not good,' said 713-DHC—the one in heels. Their voices were almost identical, but I thought 713 spoke in a minor key. 'Up means the monster.'

"'Monster?' I said. 'What monster? What's going *on* up there? Do you know?'

"The two robots looked at each other, the colored lights on their helmets flickering and blinking—*just* like the Oddity did when calculating a portal. Then they nodded in unison, a single bounce of their metal-and-glass heads, turned, and walked over to the big lamp.

"This lamp looked like a motorcar's headlight, only many, many times larger. I realized it was just like the giant searchlight I'd stood on back up in the arena, only this one was old and battered. Of course it would be, considering we were in a garbage heap.

"713-DHC went around the back, and there was a scrape of metal, and a moment later an image of their face appeared in the middle of the light. It was a bit fuzzy, but I could see how there was now a single, powerful light shining in the center of their visor. This grew and grew, until the entire lamp was whited out, and then another image appeared, projected onto the plastic shell from the inside. I watched in fascination as a sort of video began to play. It showed an empty, deserted planet, with a black sky in which a huge gold-and-purple nebula rested. Stars, impossibly close, illuminated the gas and dust, and made the night on the desert planet almost as bright as day.

"'Long, long ago,' 202-B began, and a single chord hummed in the background of their voice. 'There was a lonely planet, with no star to guide it. It floated in space, looking for a star to call home. To this planet, there came the first peoples . . . '

"Now the barren desert was suddenly populated by lanky, humanoid-mantis shapes. They scurried across the desert, and slowly, like watching a time-lapse photo, a city rose from the plain of the desert, and the gold-and-purple nebula wheeled past overhead.

"'They built cities. They built towers,' 202-B went on. 'They made music, and the planet was not lonely.'

"'Where did the people *come* from, though?' I cut in. It was a little rude, but I was so curious I couldn't help it.

"'The people came through doors, doors in the sky,' said 202-B, perfectly patient and unflustered. "They brought with them an advanced technology that allowed them to grow food from the sand and to alter the atmosphere so that it could support their life.

"'Their music floated out into space, and eventually many other species came to the planet in order to listen. Then came one who did not like the music . . .

"Now the projection showed a huge, crude ship: it was essentially a long tube with rounded ends, encrusted with little silver blobs, and eight stubby legs. One end of it had a huge, circular mouth, showing concentric rings of triangular teeth. It hovered over a city made of gleaming gold stone, and rained down fire. The city disappeared into dust, which in turn spread to envelop the whole screen, and the music in the background took on a mournful quality.

"'After that,' continued 202-B, 'the first people tried everything to make music the alien liked. Eventually, they discovered that certain voices from distant worlds would stop the alien in its tracks. But it would only listen for a single day—for the duration of one thousand songs—before it turned on the singer and devoured them.'

"The view in the lamp changed again. Now it showed a more primitive version of the arena, with a single figure dancing in the middle of it. As I watched, too stunned to say anything, the giant metal slug with the gaping mouth descended, tendrils extending from the opening, scooping up the little figure and carrying them away. The projection flickered through countless versions of this scene, as around the stage a structure took form, growing in size and complexity, until I recognized the arena where I had seen Princess Die perform.

"'But that's *horrible!*' I cried. 'Oh, and I suppose they *lure* these artists with dreams of fame and fortune. That's why they built the arena with all the cheering holograms.' Then my brain caught up with what my mouth was saying, and I looked critically at 202-B. 'Is that how *you* got tangled up in this? Why are you down here? How did you escape?'

"The image in the light flickered out, and 713 stood up and came around next to their partner. 'We did not escape,' they hummed.

"'We are the robots,' 202-B said. 'We do not care for fame and fortune. We are one with the music of the universe. Our music did not please the alien; we were rejected.'

"They didn't seem at all put out by this, and I couldn't say I blamed them.

"'*Well,*' I said, putting my hands on my hips. 'That's *something* to be going on, I suppose. How did you get hold of that nifty little video, may I ask?'

"'Many records are stored underground,' said 202-B. 'We are good listeners.'

"'I see,' I said, thinking very hard. 'Er . . . *Extrascape,* if you don't care for fame or fortune . . . how do you feel about *home?*'

"The two robots looked at me, their heads slightly tilted. They seemed puzzled.

"'Let me put it this way,' I tried again. 'If you can *help me* put a stop to this horrible, wasteful tradition, I can take you back *home.*' Oh, that looks *sugoi,* Tako-chan!"

Alister looked up with a jerk. He had been so absorbed by the Professor's tale that he'd missed the return of the octopus-man, who had arrived carrying a huge tray filled seaweed-wrapped bundles, dumplings, and little piles of pickled ginger and dollops of bright green horseradish paste—*wasabi,* he thought it was called.

There was a gurgling sound, and the blue dome of Dave's panvironment suit rolled back and Dave rose, like a little green sun, from the depths, his single orange-and-yellow eye gazing at the expanse of food in amazement.

Tako-chan set the tray carefully in the middle of the little table, took a step back, and bowed. Alister and Elo attempted to return the gesture, while Professor Odd somehow managed to bow using only her head and shoulders.

"Right," she said, once the octopus-man had left. Snapping up a pair of chopsticks she reached out and began selecting rolls and dumplings and putting them on the little plate in front of her. "There's *inari,* shrimp *nigiri,* eel, tuna and salmon *sashimi,* there's also three California-style *temaki,* one for each of us, and—I think you'll like *these* Dave—*salmon roe."* She pushed a little bowl of bright, orange-red balls toward Dave.

There was silence at the table for the next few minutes as Professor Odd devoured her serving of sushi. Alister ate slowly and experimentally. The *sashimi* was a little strange—just raw slices of fish—but the *inari* were nice, being rice wrapped in sweet tofu pouches, and the *temaki*—which was like a cone of rice wrapped in seaweed and stuffed with shrimp and avocado and dusted with sesame seeds—was surprisingly good.

The result was that Professor Odd finished long before any of them, and sat back with a sigh of satisfaction.

"That was good," she said. "Where was I? Oh, right, *Extrascape!* Well, since they were robots, and therefore reasonable, they readily agreed to help me. They had schematics for the whole complex, and we were able to take a disused maintenance elevator back to the surface. On the way, I learned a little more about them—the individual robots, I mean. It turned out they were originally part of a run of a thousand anthrobots (and numbered accordingly) meant for a variety of tasks. Each one had a characteristic, or set of characteristics, associated with them. 202-B, for example, was number 202 in the series, and B stood for either Bold or Brave or possibly both. Bold *and* Brave, I mean, not Both. Anyway, the letters behind 713 meant Decisive, Honest, and Calm—though they had changed the D to mean *Disobedient* around the time they decided they preferred making music together to . . . whatever it was they'd been programmed to do. Fascinating, really. They had such a mastery of sound, they could make music out of anything, not to mention play back all the songs they had performed out of their memory.

As we traveled up—and it took a while—I had time to think harder about what I'd learned. I began to realize that I couldn't simply whisk Princess Die away. I mean I *could* do that, yes, but it left the mantis people and that strange alien to keep on kidnapping and devouring people, which was no good. *Besides,* they were traversing universes to support this horrible practice, which meant the atrocities were multiplied accordingly! I might save *this* version of Princess Die, but what if they went after her in a *different* universe? That's the problem when you start dealing with a multiplicity of worlds—you really have to be loyal to all versions of a person, even if some of those versions don't have the history you associate with the one you first met. And there were all the *other* musicians they'd kidnapped as well. That bothered me too, because they had been *robbing* universes of these people—and not only the people, but all the creative things they might have gone on to do! Artists are influential; their creations ripple out through the population, spreading inspiration and gently shifting chances. Any one song may or may not drastically change the world, but cumulatively they are extraordinarily powerful.

"I had to put a stop to it before I tried to rescue Princess Die again. And to do that I needed to figure out what was *really* going on.

"'Look,' I told Extrascape when we were nearing the surface at last. 'Can you tap into the mainframe computer of this place? Like you did to get those histories? I need to look at more of their records.'

"'Certainly,' said 202-B, and put a hand on the nape of 713's neck. Their lights flickered in unison, and after a moment 713 said:

"'Now have complete access. Which records do you wish to see?'

"'Is there a list of all the singers they've kidnapped? All the ones that have been . . . sacrificed, that is? With what happened to them in the end, preferably.'

"'Searching,' said 713, and a little ring of lights appeared in the middle of their visor, blinking in and out so it looked like one light traveling in a circle. 'Records located. Displaying . . . '

"And they did. The circle of lights disappeared, replaced by a scrolling list of names. I recognized most of them from the file I had seen earlier, but now they were accompanied by a number, and a more detailed explanation.

"'L.B.H. Jones 1; songs: 982; status: consumed,' read the first entry. And so it went. I soon figured that the number after the name denoted which version of the person it was, the number after 'songs' was how many songs they performed, and the status was what happened to them. Almost all the song numbers were between nine hundred and one thousand, though a very few were significantly lower. Similarly, most of the entries were listed as *consumed,* though maybe a dozen were labeled *rejected.* I found Extrascape on the list: only one version, thirty songs, and *rejected.* They had by far the fewest songs, save one . . .

"Aside from Extrascape, there was only one other name with no multiples. It was M.E. Wren, and he was also the only one with just *one* song. Just one song. And he wasn't consumed *or* rejected . . . he was listed as *returned.*

"'This one,' I said, putting my finger on his name.

"'Marshal Evan Wren,' said 713. 'Human, male, home planet: Earth, 2005 A.D. Singer, songwriter, piano and geek rock.'

"'Yes, yes, I *have* heard of him—he's quite famous in some narratives. What *song* though? *What did he play?'*

"713 thought about this for a while, and finally came up with the song title: it was 'Queen of Rats.' Marshal Evan Wren sang 'Queen of Rats,' just once, and was *returned!"*

Professor Odd sat back in her seat and gazed at her audience significantly. When all she found were blank stares (and in Dave's case, some slurping sounds), she sighed heavily.

"You know 'Queen of Rats?' *They keep her bound in memories, trapped inside her own mind?"*

When Alister and Elo shook their heads, and Dave said, "I AM NOT FAMILIAR WITH THAT PIECE OF MUSIC," she rolled her head back to stare at the ceiling.

"It's a funny sort of song. Like a ballad," she explained. "Very, *very* long because of all the instrumental breaks. Its lyrics are half nonsense, half horror. Honestly I don't know what Wren was thinking of when he wrote it. Anyway, he wrote that song, and that was the song he performed in the arena, and afterward he was *returned home.* He was the *only singer* on the entire list marked as 'returned,' so naturally I got interested in the song. I'd only heard it once, though, years before, and I couldn't remember all the words.

"'Is there any way I could *see* that performance?' I asked Extrascape. 'They *must* keep records, right?'

"'Archives of the offerings are behind a lava flow,' 202-B told me. 'We cannot access without being attacked.'

"'But we remember,' 713 said. 'We remember everything.'

"And right there in the slowly rising elevator, 713 narrowed the beam of light coming out of their helmet, and projected an image on the far wall. Music emerged, too, out of the anthrobot's speakers, and though it was tinny and canned, I caught the words well enough.

"I watched Marshal Wren, standing behind an electronic keyboard, perform 'Queen of Rats' like his life depended on it. And it probably did, whether or not he realized. When the song finished at last, and the holographic crowds were still cheering distantly, a bright light shone down onto the stage, and Marshal Wren looked up, shading his eyes.

"713 must have looked up too, because the camera swung upward and *there* was the strange gun and the curling mist, and *above* that . . .

"Well, far above it all, against the bright nebula of the sky, was a creature like a huge, blocky, fat metal worm. It was covered all over with squares of metal, almost like something constructed from those interlocking plastic building bricks. From this angle I could see it had four sets of stubby feet, and instead of a face there was a circular mouth lined with teeth. This opened and closed like a diaphragm shutter, so the mouth almost looked like a giant eye at the same time.

"The huge alien bent down over the gun, and long, rope-like tendrils snaked out of its mouth-eye, twining around the contraption and rotating it so it was pointed directly at Marshal Wren. There was a noise that gave me an instant headache, a flash of light, and then Marshal Wren was gone, and the alien was drifting back up into the sky, while the stage below was suddenly swarmed with mantis people. The image blinked off, and I turned to find Extrascape looking at me curiously.

"'What is Odd planning?' asked 202-B.

"I couldn't help grinning back as I answered: 'I can *fix* this! I really can! That song is the key—oh, but I'll have to check on something first!' I was already thinking there must have been a huge misunderstanding at some point, and now I knew Marshal Wren and his silly little song were the key! I just needed to find which lock to fit it in, as it were. But I also needed to make sure that Marshal Wren actually did *go home.* So Extrascape and I had to creep through the basement of the arena, back to where I'd left the Oddity, so I could check. That was a bit tense, but they could disable surveillance cameras *literally* with a flick of their fingers, so we made it all right.

"Once we were back in the Oddity I had it do a search of all the present universes in which Marshal Wren was active. It found one that had a small blip in his history. Just the sort of blip caused by someone slipping in and out of the world. Someone not *me,* anyway. And sure enough, Marshal Wren was *still* there. Alive and well and very much still performing, too.

"I'd had to detach the Oddity from the universe with the arena to do this, so when we got back it had only been a matter of minutes, locally, even though the search had taken me hours. I'd also taken a bath and changed my clothes, and Extrascape had taught the Oddity how to play songs on her lights. She still does it, sometimes, you might have noticed. Anyway, I spent a lot of time thinking, and by the time we were ready to leave I felt I had a pretty good plan. It was a risky plan, but then any time you're dealing with a large number of militant people things are bound to get a little risky."

Professor Odd chuckled and shook her head. Then she glanced at her watch—which was the circular, flip-open kind, which she kept on a string in her pocket.

"Oh," she said. "We should probably start walking to the theater," and she waved down a passing waitress for the bill.

It turned out Tako-chan refused to accept money from them, so Professor Odd gave him a hug instead, and a light kiss on his broad forehead. Elo bowed. Dave waved. Alister said "Thank you," a bit awkwardly.

They went out the back of the restaurant and ambled down the alley toward the main street. Everyone, being rather full of fish, was moving slowly—except for Professor Odd, who skipped about as she continued to tell her story.

Part Two

"THE CONCERT—or rather, Princess Die's performance—was still going on when we got back, and the counter was reading 58/1,000. 202-B explained that they gave the performers breaks every twenty songs or so, and sure enough, after a couple more sets, some mantis people came and guided Princess Die off the stage.

"We were able to watch this happen—and read the number on the counter—because I'd been able to anchor the Oddity to a little aperture among the gun's struts and supports. It wasn't very big, and a little awkward because of the gravity difference, but it got us a great view. The only thing I couldn't see was what was going on directly above us, but judging by how many times the mantis people glanced nervously at the sky, I assumed the alien must be close.

"Once the stage was clear, I took a rope and tied it to one leg of the table and rappelled down to the net. I cut a hole in it using my sword-cane, and from there shimmied all the way down to the floor. Extrascape followed me, and by the time the mantis people returned we'd gotten ourselves sitting up on Princess Die's glittery piano; 202-B, 713-DHC, with me in the middle. I can't imagine what they thought, but Princess Die stared at us, wide-eyed, like she was really seeing things for the first time.

"Now, the first part of the plan was the riskiest, because we didn't have a good escape route, but I was fairly confident I could talk to the mantis people, since I'd managed to program the multiversal translator to work with audio. Also, Extrascape could speak the language perfectly, having had ages to listen to it.

"So when the first group of mantis people climbed up onto the stage I waved at them, and called 'Helloooooo' through my translator.

"That made them pause, so I hurried on before they could get any wrong ideas.

"'Please relax, I'm here to help. *Her,* mostly,' I said, pointing at Princess Die. 'But your lot as well. You see, I think you've gotten yourselves into a rather unfortunate situation. What with your *literal* alien overlord and all.' I pointed up, to illustrate.

"Oh yes, it *had been* the giant metal alien with the diaphragm-shutter mouth hovering over the stage that the mantis people had been glancing nervously at. It looked pretty much the same as it had on the video, only bigger and craggier. At the moment its mouth was mostly shut, just a small black circle in the center showed where it would open. But it was very tangibly *there,* looking down at the stage like some monstrous balloon animal. Every now and then little bolts of lightning would dance over its metallic skin.

"'Now look,' I went on. 'I know you think you've found a way to keep it from eating you or whatever, but I'm here to say you've *got* to stop kidnapping artists from other worlds. It's not healthy. Not for them, and not for the multiverse. So I propose you give me five minutes with Princess Die over there, and we'll see if we can't play this big guy a song that will send him away *forever.*'

"I thought I sounded pretty convincing, but I don't think the mantis people were listening very closely. What *actually* decided them was this huge, distant rumbling from above us, and the big alien's mouth began to open. Something flicked out of it, like a long narrow tongue, and almost as one the crowd of mantis people fled the stage, leaving Princess Die standing, bewildered, on her own.

"I was so worried about her—she looked ready to topple over—that I didn't see the long, gray, blade-like appendage that descended from the alien's mouth, slipping past the girders that supported the gun, until it cut through the net and crashed into the stage less than ten feet away. I hopped down off the piano and ran over to Princess Die, and before I did anything else I snapped the collar off her neck.

"She came more alive then, looked around and backed away from the debris thrown up by the alien's tongue, and then looked down at me and frowned.

"Then she said . . . well, she said some *very* rude words, but since she didn't seem angry at me I didn't mind.

"'Professor Odd, at your service,' I said, doffing my wig at her. (It was a replacement wig, orange I think.) That *really* made her look, but she came away with me willingly enough when I led her over to the piano.

"'This isn't Chicago,' she said, as if realizing it for the first time.

"'Nope,' I said, sitting her down at the bench. 'And those aren't people cheering, and this isn't a stage. Well, it sort of is, I guess. But not a stage as you would know it.'

"The tongue stabbed again, and I realized I'd have to hurry.

"I went on. 'It's a platform for people who can create a particular kind of energy. Music and words combine into something greater than the sum of their parts and pours out into the universe and—in this case—tames the big guy who's currently trying to impale us with his tongue.'

"Another stab. The only reason we hadn't been hit yet was thanks to the gun, which was blocking the alien's view of the stage.

"Princess Die looked around, then up at the huge alien. She blanched, but said, quite calmly, 'That sounds like a stage to me. So what do we do?'

"'Well, I'd like to run an experiment,' I explained. 'See, the people of this world have been using *music* to make the big metal guy in the sky not kill them. They think it's *appeasing* him or something. But *I* think something different is going on. *I* think the music has been doing something very, very different. So I'm going to try *asking him.*'

"'How?' she said. 'With your special speaking box?'

"'No,' I said, a little surprised at how well she was handling this. It was like nothing could fluster her. I think the stage could have caught fire, and she'd just calmly figure out a way to extinguish it. 'Well, *yes* I'm gonna speak with him. Her. It. Not sure what applies yet. But *first* I've got to get its attention.'

"I was interrupted at this point by another impact from the alien's blade-like tongue, and 202-B said: 'If we remain silent, we will be destroyed.'

"'*Yes*, right!' I said. 'I don't suppose you know the song 'Queen of Rats' by Marshal Wren?' I asked Princess Die.

"She frowned, and shook her head. I sighed. 'Oh well,' I said, 'I suppose I'd better sing it, then. You can play along, if you want, but Extrascape needs to do the music.'

"Princess Die peered at the two robots curiously, who were messing around in the back of the piano, making small zapping noises.

"There was a crash, and a piece of net fell down onto the stage, narrowly missing us.

"'Can I have your microphone?' I asked the Princess.

"Silently, Princess Die took off her headset and handed it to me, then reached behind her and unsnapped the little radio pack that was clipped to her belt.

"'Thanks,' I said, putting them both on. 'When you're ready, robots!'

"Now you have to imagine this scene. A huge stage, with a piano in the center of it, and on the piano are two skinny people in black leather wearing motorcycle helmets with lights on them and cables running down from their chins. One of them's wearing knee-high, stiletto-heeled boots, and the other's got a sort of metal corset thing around their waist. They're standing on the glittering piano, right? Okay, and next to them is a woman wearing a rhinestone bathing suit and platform shoes . . . and then there's *me*. I'm sort of . . . I don't actually remember. I think I was wearing my old green jacket, and of course the orange wig. But . . . I was me. And all around the edge of the stage the mantis people were crouching, and above us the net is being *shredded* by the alien's tongue. The hologram audience had flickered off, and so all the stands appeared empty. The light gun was still working, though, but the beams were random and undirected. And above all this, the giant metallic alien had rotated so it was almost vertical, with its mouth open all the way, and I looked up right at it as Extrascape began to play, and I can *see* its tongues—it had, like, five of them—poking out through the teeth, ready to strike. And *then* . . . you know what I did *then*?"

Professor Odd paused, and turned back to look at her audience expectantly. They were back on the broad thoroughfare now, and ahead, over the tops of some low buildings, Alister could see the curving roof of a huge covered stadium, lit from below by searchlights, and supporting colorful banners. On the street around them the traffic had thickened, and on the sidewalk they had been joined by a crowd of other people, most of whom were wearing elaborate costumes involving leather and glitter. It was an unusual combination.

"I can take a *guess*," Elo said.

"YOU ATTEMPTED TO COMMUNICATE WITH THE ALIEN USING MUSICAL THEORY?" Dave hazarded. Professor Odd grinned and raised a finger.

"*Very* close! Actually, I think it was the words *in* the music that did it. 'Queen of Rats,' you see, goes like this . . . "

And, to Alister's surprise, she turned around and began to sing, right there in the open, as they walked through the city. She had a full, throaty voice. Not the most pleasant to listen to, but she more than made up for it with enthusiasm and, Alister was interested to note, almost perfect diction.

"*The Queen came down today,*" she sang, waving at their fellow pedestrians who were giving her curious looks. "*She rolled her sleeves, and I heard her saaaaaaay . . . All your passions and your fears, have brought nothing but my tears! Can you keep your motions wise? Or are you ruled by what's insiiiiiiiiiide . . .* that's how it begins," she explained. "Which I think meant the alien.

The alien was the Queen, who, for some reason, was annoyed by what the mantis people were doing. If I took the song to be *completely* accurate, then I think the Queen—er, the alien—was worried that the mantis people would get caught up in their passions and lose the ability to think logically and rationally. Now, you might think that's an awful lot to read into a song that was written by someone who didn't even *belong* to that world . . . but the moment I started singing, the alien stopped trying to tear apart the stage, and hovered above us, its tongues waving back and forth to the music. Encouraged, I kept going . . .

"*Then the rats they clustered 'round, they took up trumpets from the ground. In their hearts they played and played. They sang that they were not afraaaaaaid* . . . I think those lines mean the mantis people who ignored the aliens at first, and just kept right on doing their thing—whatever it was. So the song goes on: *But the Queen she took a broom, and swept them off to their dooooooom!* That was when the alien wiped out most of the cities. *But rats are not so meek, they were back within a weeeeeek. They played at night under her bed, they put their music in her heeeeaaad* . . . that's when the mantis people started bringing in off-world musicians. *And the Queen she could not rise, but watched them dance before her eeeeeeyes!*

"This is where I started having to guess, but I took this verse to mean that the music confused the alien. Got in its head and messed it up, like the Queen in the song. Which was why the alien was stuck here. They literally *could not rise.* Anyway, next comes the bridge, which doesn't fit as well as the rest of the song, but I sang it anyway . . .

"*Oh, where have you gone? Was it something I did wrong? Where is my maddening Queen? What is it that she's seen?* Personally, I think it was things she *heard* that caused problems, but I'm getting to that. The song has a *really long* instrumental break after the bridge, and Extrascape launched into it with gusto. They'd paired themselves with the piano, which was in turn paired with the speakers, and they were playing things no human could play on that instrument. It got dissonant at times, enough to make Princess Die flinch, but when I checked, the alien's tongues were wagging almost happily, and I noticed two smaller apertures, like eyes, on either side of the huge mouth. These had been invisible till now, when they began to crack open. I fairly screamed the last verse, which was the really important bit, I thought."

"*They keep her bound in memories!*" Professor Odd fairly belted, causing the group of teenagers in fishnet stockings that were on the sidewalk ahead of them to jump and scatter. "*Trapped inside her own miiiiiind! Is it the rats she eats at night?*—that's the musicians the alien devours—*But she can't see her enemies, though they are not hard to find. They won her throne without a fiiiiiiiiiiiiiight . . .* "

Professor Odd's voice trailed off, coasting to a stop, to be absorbed by the clatter and boom of the city, and revealing the bemused muttering of the group of teenagers.

"The rats were the mantis people, of course," Professor Odd went on, unflustered. "They won the alien's throne—whatever that was—not by superior weapons, but by *driving it crazy* with the sound of music. Which isn't such a crazy notion in itself. Have you ever gotten a song stuck in your head that *wouldn't go away?* You know how *annoying* that gets? Well, imagine if that song is so fundamentally *different* from the type of music you find pleasant, it was like having a constant loop of bone-grating noise playing over and over inside your head.

"This was my theory: that the alien's preferred form of music was something so different from *ours* that what *we* found pleasant or exciting, *it found* like . . . well, like nails on a chalkboard. Which would be why the aliens attacked the mantis people in the first place. Sort of like humans who swat at flies because they find the buzzing sound annoying. Only in this case the flies came back and drove that human *mad* with the sound of their buzzing. So mad that human—er, I mean the alien—couldn't really *do* anything. Trapped inside their own mind, like the song said.

"Anyway, after I'd finished the song, and after Extrascape finished playing, I had to wait, looking up at the alien, until the little apertures opened completely and it stared down at us out of bright, glowy red eyes.

"'I'm pretty sure you can hear me,' I said, then. 'Now I've got your *attention,* listen up! I think its time you *went home* and left these people alone. Which you *can* do, if you could only *think* straight. Now, because our brains are so different, our music clearly isn't *your* music, so obviously we don't know any of your songs. But Extrascape here—' Extrascape waved '—are *very clever.* I'm sure if you, as it were, *hummed a few bars,* they could improvise something for you.'

"It was another long shot, but I guessed that hearing a bit of its own music would help clear the alien's mind. Sort of the way putting on a song you like can help your brain let go of unpleasant memories. And you know what? *I was right.*

"The alien sat there, dumbly, for a while, as all around us the mantis people went scurrying away. This was a clue, I now realize, though at the time I didn't figure out what it meant before the alien . . . well. Heh. It did exactly what I suggested: it started humming.

"It was *awful.* Worse than nails on chalkboard. Worse than those high-pitched squirrel repulsers. Like a combination of the two but with this sort of *roaring* behind it that buzzed in your teeth and made your bones itch. I think some of it was below and some *above* my range of hearing, and I'm not sure whether that made it better or worse. It was so *painful* to listen to that I tried *not* to, so I couldn't really hear the tune—if there was even a recognizable tune.

"I pressed my hands firmly over my ears, and Princess Die did the same. We both ended up on our knees on the stage, cowering together. I thought, *if* this *is what our music was like to the alien, no wonder it went mad!*

"Then Extrascape joined in, and it became almost unbearable. I tried to make myself as small as possible, to let the sound wash over me, but it just burrowed into my head and rattled around in there, like a cannonball. I couldn't move. I couldn't *think.* And that was a small mercy, I suppose, because in retrospect the whole ordeal didn't last very long—though at the time it felt like it took *forever.*

"What I remember, though, is how the pain slowly lessened, and as bits of my mind came back online I crumpled to the floor and rolled over onto my back, next to Princess Die who was doing pretty much the same thing. Together we stared up at the great, blocky metal underbelly of the alien. Little lights flashed along its side as it wheeled around, and then, its whole body undulating, it rose up into the sky, higher and higher and higher, until it was just another speck of light amid the starry nebula, and then that speck was a twinkle, and then the twinkle went out.

"It took me a while to realize that the alien had taken the horrible music with it, and that what I was still hearing was the stuff bouncing around in my own head. In an effort to push the sound out, I shoved the headset mic aside and stuck a finger in my ear—to help me hit the right notes—and sang the bridge from 'Queen of Rats' one more time.

"'*Oh, where have you gone? Was it something I did wrong? Where is my maddening Queen? What is it that she's seen?*'

"As I sang the pain lessened, and I felt a surge of relief wash over me when Extrascape—perfectly unperturbed by the whole affair—obligingly picked up the tune. Once I'd stopped singing, however, they morphed it into something new. Something slowly building with excitement, joy, and *triumph,* I realized.

"'I'm no queen,' Princess Die mumbled next to me, under the music.

"'I didn't mean you, Princess,' I replied, a little groggily.

"She sat up, rubbing her temples, and looked around.

"'Wow,' she said, dully. 'This is pretty far out. I think I'm ready to go home now.'

"That got me to sit up all at once, which made me have to put my head between my knees for a moment while my blood pressure adjusted. 'Yes,' I said, once I didn't feel dizzy anymore.

And then, when I realized what had just happened, I couldn't help letting out a little triumphant cry of my own. '*Yes!*' I said. 'We can *all* go home now!'"

Professor Odd spread her arms as they came around a corner, and there was the stadium, brightly lit and bedecked by colorful banners, the streets between them closed off with barricades and the entire place *swarming* with people. Merchants on street corners were selling t-shirts with Princess Die iconography on them, glowsticks, and little crowns with sequins. Above it all rose a huge billboard, with three faces on it. Two were motorcycle helmet-like masks, with colored lights on them. The one in the middle seemed human, but with cheekbones accentuated by prosthetic makeup, bright blue eye shadow, and long dark lashes. There was a splatter of rhinestones across the forehead, and the hair that had been sculpted into the shape of a crown above it was dyed a pale lavender. Across the bottom was written:

PRINCESS DIE: THE ROBOTS RETURN TOUR

Slowly their group slipped through the throng—Alister saw a number of people with horns, some of which looked quite real, wearing fluttery garments that glittered like morning dew—up the wide, concrete stairs, and through the vast glass doors. A wide, brown-skinned woman in a neat blue uniform took their tickets and gave them little wristbands with a bar code.

"I hope this will work for you," she said, handing one to Dave. "If not, go see the lady at information and she can make you a magnetic tag."

She didn't look twice at Elo.

"THIS WILL BE ACCEPTABLE," Dave said, curling the tip of his arm around it. "THANK YOU," he added, sounding touched.

Inside was even more crowded, and the costumes were even more magnificent. People dressed in skin-tight spandex next to people in extravagant ball gowns and people in sequined suits— with male and female representatives in each—milled around getting their pictures taken.

Professor Odd led them through the confusion with a purpose.

"It took a bit of doing to actually *get* everyone home, of course," she mentioned casually. "I was very cross with the mantis people, but when I saw how relieved they were that the alien was finally *gone*, I couldn't bring myself to berate them for how they'd handled the situation. Besides, that might have made them hostile again, and I wanted their help sending everyone home, since it would have taken *forever* using just the Oddity. But they were really quite a *reasonable* race, once they had the threat of sudden annihilation by giant alien removed, and they started up their own transuniversal machine without much fuss.

"I took Princess Die home myself. I could tell she was getting tired of the whole thing, and since Extrascape didn't seem too keen on staying either I loaded them all up into the Oddity—after I'd moved the portal to somewhere more easily accessible—and took everyone back to Princess Die's world. I'd thought after that I'd find a nice place for Extrascape to settle down, since they didn't want to go back to their native universe, but Princess Die had gotten very interested in them, and by the time I'd got the portal to her hotel room open, they had decided to give her world a try.

"'It'll be *amazing*,' she told them as they tumbled out into her suite. "*Real* robots—people won't believe it! I hope you don't mind being mistaken for guys in suits? I don't know if this world is ready for musical androids.'

"'Anthrobots,' 202-B corrected her.

"'Yeah, sure,' said Princess Die.   'Do anthrobots drink scotch? What about you . . . um . . . ?'

"'Professor Odd,' I reminded her. 'And no, I really shouldn't. Must get back and see all the other musicians are returned properly. I mean, they probably *will* be . . . but you can't be too careful.'

"She asked me if I would be going then. I said yes. She told me to come back and see her sometime. I got very flustered at that and hurried away without really saying anything. I *had* intended to go back, after I'd sorted the other musicians out . . . but . . . well . . . that took *longer* than I thought it would, and by then I really needed some sleep. And after that I decided I wanted a holiday, which was the first time I went to Geda, I think, and you know how *that* turned out. And after that there were the Rats of Alnitak, and then I got really interested in testing the event horizons of black holes and . . . well . . . one thing led to another and by the time I'd worked up the courage to go back, the Oddity's temporal lock had slipped and enough time had passed that I wasn't sure if Princess Die would even *remember* me . . .

"I did check in though, of course. Just to see how they were doing. Things got a bit rough for Princess Die—she spent six months in rehab, and everyone said her career was over. It was reported as a combination of anorexia and alcoholism, but I think it was post-traumatic stress from her ordeal. But she got through it, and went back on tour—*with* Extrascape as her opening act. Did very well from then on, and Extrascape eventually became quite famous in their own right. That's why I was so excited to catch *this* show. It's the first time they've performed together in five years. Oh, and Extrascape are out as *real* anthrobots now, so I'm excited to see what they do."

"You'll like it," said the usher who checked their ticket stubs and pointed the way down a hall to their seats. He was a young man with dark skin and black hair and an earnest look about him. He had clearly only caught the last few words of Professor Odd's monologue.

"It's their *first time* at a Princess show," Professor Odd told him, giddily.

"Ah," said the young man knowingly. "Well, you're in for a *treat*. You're down near the arena, by the way—they have a ramp to the left if you can't do stairs," he added, obviously for Dave's benefit.

"THANK YOU, I AM SURE I WILL MANAGE," Dave said as he rolled past. The young man didn't even blink.

"Hold on, hold on," said Alister, once they were a safe distance down the hall. It was much less crowded here—most people either being outside milling around, or already seated—but his voice echoed loudly. "You mean to say you just dropped Princess Die off and *never went back to explain things?* Just left her at home as if . . . as if the whole thing was a big, weird *dream?*"

"One that she came out of with a pair of musical robot friends?" Elo added.

Professor Odd wiggled her shoulders uncomfortably. "It just . . . didn't feel *right* . . . barging in, I mean. I mean, I don't *really* know her. I just like her music. A *lot*. But she doesn't know *me* at all. I'm just this weird person who helped her out once—and I can't imagine what she's made of it all. She was pretty out of her mind for most of it. She probably doesn't remember me. Not really. It would be *weird*."

Alister gazed at Professor Odd an astonishment, while behind him Elo burst out:

"Weird? Since when have *you* been afraid of things being *weird?*"

"I felt *shy,* if you *must* know!" Professor Odd cried out, turning on them in a whirl of shiny orange coat. She took a deep breath, her chest swelling up like a pigeon's. "And I get very nervous meeting famous people. Famous people I admire, anyway." She turned on her heel and marched down the hall, turning off at the door labeled "Arena Level, A 030–060."

Checking his ticket stub, Alister saw it was indeed labeled "AL A 042" and he followed the Professor, but not before exchanging an eye-roll with Elo. Dave, impassive in his panvironment suit, trundled after them.

They encountered the promised stairs immediately, and Dave surged ahead of them by tipping sideways and rolling his barrel-shaped suit down them, using the gear around his midsection as a brace. He was waiting for them at the bottom, where there was another usher who, after a peek at their stubs, pointed to their right.

They came out around a buffer and there *was* the arena: the center of the stadium, one half built up into an elaborate stage like a spaceship, with the other half bare concrete packed with people. A living chain made of security guards ringed them in, and a small fence further separated the arena from the first row of seats. Once they reached AL A 039-042 and sat down, Alister found he was more or less at eye level with the lowest part of the stage. He was about as far away from it as one would be from the screen of a movie theater if they sat in the very back row, but after leaning around to gaze at the hundreds of rows of seats stretching up and behind them, he realized what good seats these really were. Only the people standing on the floor got closer to the stage, and Alister suspected they didn't have as good a view.

The stage itself was something to behold. There was a big semicircle that jutted out into the throng of people, and behind it was a bank of computer screens with little blinking lights and dials. The screens were playing computer-generated animations of nebulas, supernovas, and solar eclipses. Above this were two pods, large enough to hold a grown man, which were belching fog. They each had large letters stenciled across the lid, which spelled out CRYO. Between them was a chair—clearly meant to be the captain's chair—which stood empty. Beyond this the stage rose in a complicated framework of ramps and ladders and poles and catwalks, to where it was swallowed up by a rich, black velvet curtain.

"Here," said Professor Odd, pressing something small and soft into Alister's hand. He looked down to find a pair of yellow foam earplugs resting in his palm.

"Trust me, you'll need them," the Professor said with a grin, working a pair into her own ears.

"Gosh, *thanks,*" said Elo, putting on a pair of sound-dampening headphones.

"I AM GRATEFUL I HAVE MY OWN SYSTEM OF HEARING," Dave announced, garnering a surprised look from their neighbors in seats 43 and 44. But the couple appeared more interested in taking pictures of the stage than the strange robot-like creature, and looked away again quickly.

After a while a voice boomed out of the high, vaulted ceiling, its words lost in its own echo and the roar of the crowd as everyone in the stadium—which had filled to capacity—began to scream. Everyone except Alister, Elo and Dave, who winced as Professor Odd jumped to her feet, sticking two fingers in her mouth and whistling loudly.

The voice spoke again, and now Alister saw how the lights on the stage were flickering wildly, sparks flying from a few places further up among the catwalks. Lithe figures in black leotards could be seen, jumping and climbing and running about up there, and the two cryo pods had been lit from within to reveal a dark, humanoid figure in each.

Listening carefully, Alister was able to discern words in the echoes this time around.

"Ladies and gentlemen and everyone between and beyond, robots, monsters and aliens . . . " the booming voice said. "Are you ready for *Extrascape?*"

Tremendous cheers, interspersed with beeps and whistles and some horrible screeching.

"Are you ready . . . for *Princess Die?*"

The noise, if possible, increased. Alister was glad of his earplugs.

"They have come a long way . . . " said the voice, over the cheering which refused to die down, " . . . from a galaxy beyond your imagination! Our Princess has returned from a journey of discovery, and she brings with her the envoys of a new age. An age of acceptance, an age of life! An age of revolution! Evolution! But most of all . . . an age"—something boomed, and a searchlight blazed upward, illuminating the rolling bank of stage fog—"of song! And! *Dance!*"

On the final word there was a huge clash of cymbals and a figure appeared, as if by magic, in the middle of the clear semicircle. For a moment they were enveloped in a pillar of golden light, and then the next their form solidified into a tall, slender woman wearing an elaborate platinum costume full of spikes and odd angles. She looked like she was wearing a giant crystal.

"*Ooohh-ooohh-oooooooooh-ooh-oh, oh, oh, calling Professor Odd* . . . " sang the woman.

Alister nearly choked in surprise.

But he hadn't heard wrong. The woman repeated:

"*Ooohh-ooohh-oooooooooh-ooh-oh, oh, oh, calling Professor Odd!*"

Alister turned to stare at Professor Odd, his mouth agape.

"How *can* she not have remembered you?" he shouted over the din of music, cheering, and singing. "She put you in a bloody *song!*"

"It's just what she *thought* I was," Professor Odd said, a small, wistful smile spreading across her face. "What she remembered . . . "

From what Alister caught of the lyrics, he thought Princess Die must have remembered things remarkably well. There was a line about *"who has the answers I want to believe, who has a citrus wig of maple and bees . . . "* that seemed pretty accurate. Except for the bit about the maple and bees, which Alister put down to a case of mishearing.

Then Extrascape came out of their pods, and he forgot to listen to the lyrics for a couple minutes.

They did look remarkably like tall, thin people in leather suits with helmets on, but there was a jaggedness about their bodies, and a precision to their movements, that seemed just a little *off*. Their proportions were neither classically male, nor classically female, though 202-B appeared shorter and curvier, because of the corset it wore, and 713-DHC looked taller, because of the high heels. Their helmets were alight with colors and their hands glinted metallically. They marched down the steps to the lowest part of the stage, where a small panel had risen, and stood behind it. Almost at once the music redoubled, taking on subtle electronic undertones, and both the robots nodded their heads to the beat of the music. The crowd went wild.

When Alister could again hear what Princess Die was singing, he began to realize that the song wasn't *just* about Professor Odd (or, Professor Odd as Princess Die had perceived her). It also seemed to be about Princess Die's *feelings* about Professor Odd, if the lines *"When I'm lonely I just have to pretend that through the door is Professor Odd,"* and *"When I'm so low and everything seems wrong, I will try to find Professor Odd,"* meant anything. There was the continued refrain of *"Call-*

ing Professor Odd," interspersed with shouts of *"Want Professor Odd!"*

Then Extrascape began to chant, quickly, and without breaks to breathe, *"Onwards fusion-crazy, who's like a supernova—onwards fusion-crazy, who's like a supernova . . . "* for at least a minute, while the music did funny things in the background, and Princess Die danced, until they closed with: *"Onwards crashing-crazy, crossed wires can't delete you, baby."*

"She's like a star, made up of all your dreams," Princess Die took over. *"She's like a star, she's burning through the screams . . . "* and then went off into a language Alister didn't recognize. When the lyrics returned to English it was to repeat, *"She's burning through the screams, made up of all your dreams—my technicolor sta-a-ar, she's Professor Odd!"*

And then some words jumped out at him, from the midst of the music, the cheering, and the echoing refrain, *"Stuck on a stage, trapped in the thousand songs, I know I can call Professor Odd . . . "*

Alister wanted to jump up and *shake* Professor Odd. It was *obvious* that Princess Die remembered, and from the sound of the song, she was probably *still missing* her. But he restrained himself until the music finished (*"Don't want drugs and fame, this fame's not a game. Won't worship your rod, want Professor Odd!"*), and he had a chance of actually being heard.

"How can you think she doesn't remember?" Alister screamed. "She's practically *pining* after you!"

"She's just trying to make sense of some very conflicting memories!" Professor Odd shouted back through the roar of the crowd.

On the stage, Princess Die had joined hands with Extrascape and was leading them forward to the edge, saying something along the lines of how *glad* she was to be back in San Jose with her very best robot friends—who were now able to be out of their helmets, as it were, about being *actual* robots.

"Professor," said Alister, trying to sound cross, even though inwardly he found the whole situation tragically hilarious. "If you don't go visit her *right* after the show is done, I shall be very, *very* disappointed! Forget being a fangirl for once—you *owe* it to her! *And* Extrascape!"

"I could talk to Extrascape," Professor Odd allowed, but she crumpled back into her seat and mumbled something else.

Alister pulled out his earplugs. "*What?*" he said.

"She's so *very* busy these days," Professor Odd repeated testily. "And I'm sure she'll be *exhausted* after the performance. I wouldn't want to bother her."

"I *really* don't think you'll be a bother—" Alister began, but one of the people in the row behind them had leaned down and was making annoyed *shushing* motions with their hands. Alister sat back reluctantly, but he caught sight of Elo waving at him from the far side of the Professor, and he left his earplugs out long enough to hear her say:

"Don't worry! If she won't do it, *I'll* open a portal into Die's dressing room *myself!*"

"You wouldn't—!" Professor Odd began, but at that moment the next song started up, and their conversation was cut off.

Alister passed the rest of the concert in a state of growing admiration. The trio performed song after song after song, some of which went on for a long time. Princess Die went through about five variations on her original costume, played a piano made of crystal, danced on the piano in five-inch heels, and at one point was lifted clean into the air by a set of ropes. Extrascape spent most of their time behind their little control panels, manipulating pieces of the set along with the music. The dancers in black crawled all over it, coming down to dance with Princess Die now and then. There were some slow songs, some fast songs, and some songs that went back and forth.

Princess Die's lyrics seemed to be rather complicated with a lot of hidden meanings. Alister wished he knew the secret to them. They seemed, to him, to be parts of a bigger narrative, and if he only knew the secret to the code they were written in he could understand that story. As it was he contented himself with enjoying the music, an interesting blend of orchestral rock and roll merged with Extrascape's electronic tunes.

There were a couple of breaks where Princess Die paused and talked to the audience, or talked to Extrascape. She went down to the edge of the stage to receive a gift from one of the people on the floor, and came back holding a rhinestone-studded vest with the words "woman of thunder" picked out on the back. She thanked the fan profusely, getting a little teary as she did so.

"Fans are so, *so* important," she said, putting the vest on. "You all probably know how I hit a low spot maybe a decade ago—right before I met Extrascape. I was a real mess, and it was a bad time. People said I was done. Washed out. A loser. But my fans always believed in me. It was my *fans* who got me through it, they really did. I wouldn't be here today without you, my fans."

Alister had to roll his eyes at Professor Odd, but he didn't think she noticed; she was watching the stage, enraptured.

The concert went on. Alister lost track of the songs—though he didn't think there were actually a thousand of them. Then it finished, but the people stayed and kept cheering. So Princess Die came back and did a solo piece, just her and the piano in the middle of an empty stage. After that there was still *more* cheering, so Extrascape came back and lit up the whole stage with their music. And then, when people still wouldn't go, they *both* came back and did a song together. This one was markedly different from all the other songs, and seemed a little off the cuff. Princess Die broke down laughing several times, and would pause to talk to the audience, telling them over and over how much she enjoyed playing for them. Extrascape did too, in their own way—though their words were woven in with the music, and Alister had trouble distinguishing them.

And then, at last, Extrascape and Princess Die left the stage, the house lights went up, and people began, reluctantly, to filter out.

"Right," said Alister, standing up and taking Professor Odd's elbow in a loose hold.

"Right," said Elo, doing the same on the other side.

"This is absolutely ridiculous," Professor Odd protested.

"I COULDN'T AGREE MORE," said Dave, as he followed the three of them out of the stadium.

Epilogue

PRINCESS DIE STRETCHED OUT as much as the tiny dressing room would allow. One would think that a venue as huge as the stadium in San Jose would also have a comfortable dressing room, but all the space had been spent on room for the stage and the audience, with almost nothing left for the artists and the crew.

This was all right for Extrascape, who just leaned themselves against the wall over their portable chargers and went into sleep mode, but Princess Die, despite her myriad stage personas of aliens, demons, gynoids, and metaphysical deities, was in reality only human—and not even a very young one anymore.

"I think I need a bath . . . of ice," she croaked, sipping at the tall glass of water that had replaced her traditional post-concert whisky since . . . well . . . since she'd met Extrascape.

Princess Die was a practical woman, and as such did not look too closely at the jumble of foggy memories she had of her "crash" as the press had called it. And she had crashed. Badly. Been right off the rails for a few months. Hadn't known what to think or what was real. There were memories of a strange, clicking language, and other, weirder things. She'd ended up putting them all into the song "Professor Odd" and then only thought about them when she performed it.

She was still thinking about it now, however, as she rolled the remaining water around in her glass, wishing it was something stronger.

"Who has the answers I want to believe?" she whispered.

There was a scratch on her door.

Princess Die leaned her head back and shut her eyes. She'd asked Carol, her tour manager, for ten minutes of absolute solitude, and she knew she still had six more to go.

"What is it?" she called, tiredly.

To her surprise it wasn't the main door that opened, but the little closet door next to it. A dark crack appeared, and from the other side were voices. Princess Die caught the words, "*. . . really a very bad idea . . .*" and "*. . . that never stopped you before!*" and then a furry, golden head pushed itself through the crack and looked around.

It looked like a dog. Or a wolf. Except it was too intelligent, and far too high off the ground. Princess Die had seen a lot of strange things since the convergence, but this was possibly the most surprising.

A humanoid wolf with gleaming, buttery-golden fur, wearing a purple jumpsuit, slid out of her closet and bowed apologetically.

"So sorry to bother you, princess," the dog said in perfect, slightly British-sounding English. "Only, it seemed like the best time. I'm sure you'll understand." Then she poked her head back through the door and called, "Better give her a push, Alister!"

"There's really no need for that," said a voice from within Princess Die's closet. It was the same as the first voice, and it sparked memories, distant as dreams.

A moment later the memories got a lot less distant when Professor Odd pushed her way out of the closet and past the golden wolf.

Princess Die knew it was Professor Odd at once, even though the woman was wearing a bright orange overcoat, and her wig was a swirl of orange and pink and blue. It was the same shaggy, flyaway cut that her previous one had been. The tentacle that she remembered, but hadn't had the courage to put in the song, was curled tightly under the woman's jaw, and her eyes were very large and dark. Like a cat's.

"So *sorry* about this," she was saying, pulling at the ends of her lime-green scarf. "I didn't want you bother you—know you must be tired. But they *insisted* I check in on you—and I wanted to say hello to Extrascape anyway . . . "

That was the voice. A little raspy, but so animated and *earnest.* Princess Die realized she was staring at her visitor with her mouth slightly open, utterly astonished.

Over by the wall, Extrascape whirred into life, the lights on their helmets running through the boot-up sequence.

There was a knock on the door. A real knock this time, on the real door, and a moment later Carol put his head in.

"Ten minutes, Die," he said. "I've got the very polite writer for *NewWire* dot com, also Johnny Bathory's manager called, asking if—" he cut off at the sight of Professor Odd and the wolf. "Oi!" he said, his normally bluff, pleasant face clouding over. "What are you—"

"*Not now*, Carol," Princess Die said, trying and failing to sound casual. But she didn't want to take her eyes off Professor Odd, lest the woman disappear on her again, and so her words came out rather sharp.

Carol, bless him, took the hint and backed out of the door, shutting it diffidently behind him.

*   *   *

The door shut with a clap, leaving Professor Odd to stare back at Princess Die almost defiantly. From his post on the stairs, blocking Professor Odd's retreat back into the Oddity, Alister saw a pair of long legs in fishnet tights swing off the little makeup table, and a moment later Princess Die advanced into view between Elo and the Professor.

Alister had to marvel at how, though the two women were of similar height and build, the closer you got to Professor Odd, the stranger she looked, but the closer you looked at Princess Die the more normal she seemed. She had a scattering of moles around her collarbone, and the backs of her thin hands were a little wrinkly. She was maybe in her mid-to-late-thirties, and that age showed rather more now that she had most of her makeup off.

Her face was also more expressive this way, and Alister saw her eyes widen, her mouth opened in a disbelieving "*oh.*"

"You're real," she said in a small, hollow voice.

"*Yep,*" said Professor Odd, wiggling her shoulders awkwardly.

Princess Die nodded to herself, and when Alister saw the small, triumphant grin spread across her face, he couldn't help feeling immensely pleased with himself.

"You saw the show?" Princess Die asked, almost hesitantly.

"Oh," said Professor Odd, clearly taken aback. "Oh *yes!* Yes it was *brilliant!*"

Elo coughed. "I'll just, er, I'll just *wait for you outside,* shall I?" she asked, then waved a paw at Princess Die's protesting expression. "You lot have *loads* to catch up on, I'm sure," she said, backing toward the door as she spoke. "Don't mind us. We'll wait. Have fun."

So saying she shut the Oddity's door with a quiet click.

In the tiny dressing room, Princess Die regarded Professor Odd curiously.

"I hope you don't mind if I ask the obvious, obnoxious question first," she said. "But . . . just who in the world *are* you?"

Professor Odd smiled, a little cryptically. "I'm just a *fan,* Princess Die. One of the many. Never underestimate the importance of a good fan base. But, to be honest, I think that lovely song you wrote does as good a job describing me as anything I could say."

"The Odd is back?" asked 713, their lights blinking fiercely.

"Odd is back," announced 202-B. They regarded Professor Odd critically. "You have lost your cane," they said.

"*Ah,*" said Professor Odd, turning around in the little room. For lack of a chair, she went and sat on a bundle of gymnastics mats that had been stuffed into a corner. "That's a rather long story . . . "

Alister and Elo and Dave sat up around the table for a few hours, but eventually they gave up waiting and went to bed. Alister was woken at some point, hours later, by the soft sound of singing coming from downstairs. Putting his head through his door, he looked down to find Professor Odd had returned, and that it was she who was singing. She'd lost her orange jacket, but had acquired a tuxedo-like coat with rhinestones on the tail, and her rainbow wig had been exchanged for a lavender one with long tresses pinned into a complicated hairdo like piles of whipped cream. Alister recognized it as one of Princess Die's signature wigs.

"How'd it go?" he called down.

Professor Odd looked up at him. She seemed a little wobbly. She grinned.

"It's *so* nice," she said. "It's so, *so* nice when artists really *appreciate* their fans." She climbed up the ladder and tottered over to her room, still singing softly . . .

"When you're lonely you just have to pretend beyond that door is Professor Odd. You're not a looney, you can go tell your friends that you can call on Professor Odd . . . "

FURTHER READING

This is the tenth novella of Professor Odd. The next adventure can be found in:

PROFESSOR ODD #11:

DAVEBOT

ABOUT THE AUTHOR

Goldeen Ogawa is a writer, illustrator and cartoonist. She lives in California where she writes stories, draws pictures, and takes care of various animals. She originally wanted to be an actor, but upon finding all the good parts were for men, she took a break from the stage to write some stories with parts she would like to play.

The project is currently ongoing.

Her official website and blog is at

www.goldeenogawa.com.

TEXT AND DESIGN

The body of this book was typeset using LaTeX in Carter Sans.

Cover art and book design by the author.

www.ingramcontent.com/pod-product-compliance
Lightning Source LLC
Chambersburg PA
CBHW070537130626
46555CB00003B/1465